IN THE WHITE

BY AMBER TAYLOR

An absurdist mystery, raising funds for struggling theatre companies during the COVID – 19 pandemic and to help assist with the 2020 Yemen Crisis.

To whoever holding this!

Thank you so, so much for this, it means the world – not only to myself but to the many people benefitting from your donation and purchase.
100% of all royalties and profits from the sale of this script will be split evenly between two causes that I care about deeply. The first, being the 2020 Yemen crisis. If you are unaware of the situation, I urge you to spare some time and research just how badly people are suffering. At the point of this publication, Yemen is the largest humanitarian crisis in the world, with more than 24 million people in need of humanitarian aid and assistance. Your donation will help provide sanitation, basic food supplies and resources to those suffering the most. It will also help on the ground support – providing PPE and equipment to those risking their lives to help. Thank you.

The second is in wake of the 2020 Covid-19 pandemic. Whilst help from the U.K government has only just been provided; it is not enough to help struggling theatre companies remain above water. Those most at risk of closure, redundancies and collapse are smaller, local organizations, particularly those supporting disabled, LGBTQ+, low-income and ethnic minority performers. Your donation will go straight to independent companies and help make sure this important art form is preserved and protected, not just for future generations but also for the present ones. Thank you.

Lastly, I really hope you enjoy the play and would love to hear any feedback! Likewise if you'd like to learn more about these causes or keep up to date with the scripts progress, I'd love to talk! At the time of this publication I can be contacted via email (AmberTaylor024@gmail.com) or Instagram (@amber_1307_)

Again, from the bottom of my heart, thank you!

-A

Oh! And a little thank you to those who have stuck beside me through all my 3am writing breakdowns and highs! Gemma Satherley – Thomas - my right arm. My Co-director and crutch, Tom Wilson. Llantwit + Lancaster girlies. LUTG who gave it a home. Anyone who ever helped me with the dreaded first edit. And of course, my beautiful family. I owe you so much x

Character list

For inclusivity reasons, two of the four characters have been purposely left ungendered, with no reference to age, race or ethnicity. It is solely down to the reader, audience or performers and directing team how they are imagined.

NONNA

MITTY

THE WOMAN

THE INDIVIDUAL

ACT ONE - *Scene One*

(The room is too clean. Too pristine. And everything, is too white.

It is an almost bare, average-sized space with enough room for a dance or small gathering - but that is not its primary function. Surrounded by only darkness, this room is purely for living. In the centre is a white Sofa, placed behind a thick, white woollen rug and adjacent to an equally bland wall.

The floor is neither littered with the toys of a child, nor are the walls adorned with family photos or artwork, and as for the source of light - it comes from far above - flooding the room and basking it in a harsh ray which is comfortable for living, but that is all.
However, the uncomfortable cleanliness of the room is overlooked by the three figures positioned in the space - and even more so by their actions.

*The first, **NONNA**, is a charming, youthful epitome of human curiosity - almost dripping with creativity and childlike innocence. Nonna sits, dressed in white and cross- legged at the front, staring animatedly forward and not blinking for unhuman amounts of time.*

*The second - **MITTY** -is also not seated upon the Sofa, but rather sits to the side of it. Back pressed flat against the arm of the Sofa and poised forward, reading a white, untitled book. Also dressed in white, Mitty is a level-headed, older, almost sad being of pure intelligence.*
As for the last inhabitant, little can be understood or translated from its strange pose. It has sprawled itself against the back wall, face pressed as tightly as possible against it - away from the audience - as if trying to melt into the cement. As slow seconds start to pass, the limbs of this figure caress and stroke the wall, searching for a bump or imperfection which will never come. After realizing this, the figure slowly folds in on itself, twisting and descending until it crawls into a ball and faces away from the rest of the room.

A long silence ensues.

*Slowly **NONNA** begins to hum and rock very slowly back and forth, eyes staying as transfixed as ever. As she laughs gently, **MITTY** shuts the novel annoyed, and looks over puzzled.)*

MITTY: Nonna… What are you looking at exactly?

NONNA: *(Staring forward, smiling gently)* A metaphor.

MITTY: *(Sighs)* Not again.

NONNA: Want to hear it?

MITTY: No.

(Pause)

NONNA: But wasn't it you who taught me the process of metaphorical intake?

MITTY: Yes, but-

NONNA: So, don't you want to see the results of your excellent teaching?

MITTY: Yes but -

NONNA: - And wasn't it you who told me that metaphors are designed to share?
MITTY: *(Frustrated)* Yes, but so are STD's Nonna! Just leave me alone.

(Pause)

NONNA: Are you sure?

MITTY: *(Through gritted teeth)* Later, I'm busy.

NONNA: You don't look busy.

MITTY: You're not looking at me, how would you know?

NONNA: Well how do you know *you're* not busy? You're not looking at yourself either…

(Laughs)

Oh. Wait. I forgot. You're always looking at yourself, you narcissistic -

MITTY: - Fine!... Fine. What's the stupid metaphor?

(Nonna pats the ground. Mitty sighs and begrudgingly moves to sit at the front. Unsatisfied with the proximity, Nonna pats the ground again and Mitty rolls his eyes, moving an inch closer. Nonna suddenly points out towards the audience and gestures happily.)

NONNA: Look at the metal. Right out there… See it? Look at the way it crosses and runs alllll the way up, parallel like a train track.

MITTY: That's not a metaphor. Have I taught you nothing?

NONNA: Just wait for it…… the metal………. the train track...... is a metaphor for the middleman and capitalism.

MITTY*: (Scoffs)* What?

NONNA: Well see it this way, the third rail is electrified at 1200 volts, are you following?
MITTY: Yes.

NONNA: Well that's kind of lethal right? Almost like the middleman. Following?

MITTY: I'm following a bloody lunatic.

(Nonna hears and Mitty receives a sharp dig to the side.)

Ow! Yes, yes... I'm following, I'm following!
Please…please…continue to illuminate my intelligence.

(Gestures and rolls eyes)

NONNA: *(Excitedly at speed)*

See it this way, capitalism thrives off the middleman, the middleman thrives off capitalism. Almost like how the train needs the track to continue its journey but the track also needs the train in order to exist. But also, if anyone wanted to disrupt the cycle of the trains journey, they'd need to remove the third rail, but they can't because they'll get electrocuted and die.

(Giggles breathlessly)

See?

MITTY: *(Pauses to digest the information, a bit baffled)*

So…you're saying that capitalism will continue because it thrives on middlemen… and if anyone tries to remove the middleman, they'll die?

NONNA: No Mitty, I'm merely saying words. *(Laughs and taps Mitty's head)* Your brain is translating it and telling you that capitalism will continue because it thrives on-

MITTY: *(Annoyed)* - Wait, so you're saying you interrupted my perfectly, intellectual train of thought to tell me all that nonsense? *(Nonna chuckles)* And then you tell me the metaphor wasn't even – Why are you laughing?

NONNA: You said train of thought, I thought considering the topic we were previously discussing it was quite humorous.

MITTY: I hate you. *(returns to previous seat)*

(Pause)

I have a metaphor

NONNA: Ooh go on.

MITTY: Our names.

NONNA: Not following.

MITTY: Think of them together.

NONNA: *(Confused but enthralled)* What, Mitty and Nonna?

MITTY: No flip them round.

NONNA: *(Tries to say them backwards, spelling out the words in mid-air)*

y…. tt…im and ann…on?

MITTY: No, you fool. I meant flip which word you say first.

NONNA: Oohh… right... um Nonna and Mitty!

MITTY: Now say it really fast.

NONNA: Nonnamitty

MITTY: Get it?

NONNA: No.

MITTY: It's like Anonymity! You know the noun?

NONNA: That's not a metaphor.

MITTY: Yes, it is.

NONNA: No, a metaphor is saying something is something when its clearly not.

Like… Love is a battlefield.

MITTY: *(Pointedly)* Yes… and I'm saying our names are a conspiracy.

NONNA: (*Looks concernedly at Mitty*)

Are you feeling okay?

MITTY: I feel great, if I had a tail, I'd wag it. Look, you're overlooking the important thing here which is-

NONNA: (*Rolls eyes*) Our names are not a conspiracy Mitty.

MITTY: (*Suspiciously*) They are. Why else would we have been paired? All my past colleagues have had normal names.

NONNA: But Nonna is a normal name!

MITTY: (*Shakes head in doubt*) Maybe you're a part of it, I bet you are.

NONNA: (*Laughs*) You've finally cracked haven't you.

(Pause)

MITTY: (*Suspiciously*) You know something, don't you?

NONNA: Mitty we never leave this place! I'm always here by your side. Don't you think you'd notice if things were up?

I thought you were meant to be the smart one.

MITTY: I am the smart one.

(Huffs)

I suppose… I suppose you're right. I guess by now I know you for what you truly are.

NONNA: Which is?

MITTY: A witty fool.

NONNA: *(Grins)* Better that than a foolish wit.

MITTY: Shakespeare wrote that, right?

NONNA: I can't remember.

MITTY: *(Admiringly)* Now that's a man who worked with metaphors if ever I saw one.

(Pause)

NONNA: I thought he worked up in HR.

MITTY: We don't have a HR! Why do you have to make a joke out of everything? It's like working with a child!

NONNA: It's better than being miserable all the time!

MITTY: You can't make a joke about everything you know.

NONNA: I can.

(Pause)

MITTY: You know…You're like a Russian doll.

NONNA: How so?

MITTY: Too damn full of yourself.

(Nonna shoots Mitty an annoyed look, stands and heads to the Sofa. Mitty looks up and tries to figure out what's happening.)

MITTY: What are you doing now?

(Nonna ignores Mitty and starts searching down the back of the Sofa. A moment passes before a packet of cigarettes is triumphantly found.)

NONNA: *(Opens cigarettes and puts one to mouth. Taking a drag, Nonna throws the pack to Mitty, who catches them disgusted.)*

To good health!

MITTY: *(Pushes the packet away and rolls eyes)*

'Good health' is merely the slowest rate at which one can die.

NONNA: *(Shrugs)* To bad health then!

MITTY: You do know we can't actually die? Well not from age or disease anyway.

NONNA: I don't. Have you tried?

MITTY: Tried what?

NONNA: Dying. You should give it a go sometime.

(Nonna looks over at the figure in a ball at the back of the room.)

She's doing my head in.

MITTY: She's doing nothing.
NONNA: Exactly.

MITTY: A little ironic don't you think? It's not like we're doing anything either…

NONNA: Yes, we are. We're doing our jobs.

MITTY: True.

(The two return to their original opening positions - Mitty, back to the side of the Sofa and Nonna sat, staring out into the audience.

The mysterious figure at the back slowly stands and repeats the same movements as before. But this time each move is slightly more desperate, pressing into the wall with such strength it may fall, arms caressing, pushing and dropping as if the wall will run away for good. As the movements increase in intensity, the figure suddenly stops, looks down at the floor and breathes in exasperatedly. Very slowly, they turn, and we get a first look at the tear and mascara stained face of an aging, skinny woman. Tears pour from her eyes, but she is almost expressionless; Any noticeable emotion is one of pain. She puts a hand back on the wall and trails it down until she curls back up, facing away from the audience. Nonna continues staring at the world but this time is noticeably anxious and concerned.)

MITTY: Nonna… What are you looking at exactly?

NONNA: *(Pauses, not breaking eye contact when answering.)*

A metaphor.

MITTY: Not again.

NONNA: Want to hear it?

MITTY: No.

(Pause)

NONNA: Are you sure?

MITTY: Later I'm busy.

(A long silence)

NONNA: *(Toneless, staring out into the darkness, hollowly)*

Mitty, I keep having dreams.
MITTY: *(Chuckles)* Well, with your work ethic, I doubt they'll be coming true anytime soo-

NONNA: (*Is trance like, still staring*)

Mitty... I don't think they're dreams.

MITTY: Well make your mind up.

NONNA: Mitty, I'm scared.

(*Suddenly very tense and concerned, Mitty looks sharply at Nonna and stands up warily. After a second of looking, Mitty cautiously walks over to Nonna.*)

MITTY: That's new.

NONNA: (*Shaking, very scared*)

Mitty... I... I don't know what going to happen.

MITTY: Stop this.

NONNA: (*Sways a little, becoming nauseous, grabs on to Mitty to remain steady*)

Mitty...

MITTY: Stop this! Nonna Stop! You know what they'll do! Stop this for goodness sake!

NONNA: I.... I can't Mitty... I can't... (*Shows a shaking hand*)

MITTY: (*Shakes Nonna*) Nonna snap out of this.

This instance!

(*Mitty takes a step back, then notices the Woman behind has stood, watching expressionlessly.*)

What are you looking at? Leave us alone!

(The Woman doesn't react, angering Mitty. Nonna, who has been staring forward, suddenly sits, drawing knees to chest and starts rocking fearfully back and forth)

MITTY: *(To Woman)*

Leave Us Alone!

(Looks around exasperatedly then to Nonna)

Nonna, you must stop this! You're not supposed to be like this!

(Nonna rocks faster and faster, deaf to Mitty's attempts to calm the situation. Mitty looks around for a solution then stops, hands clasped behind head, stressfully considering something. Then with a swift action Mitty slaps Nonna hard in the face)

Nonna, stop!

(Mitty looks down at Nonna, who slowly sits up, back to normal and nursing where Mitty hit. With a sigh of relief, Mitty sits back down. The Woman lowers herself back to the floor.)

MITTY: *(Breathless)* What the hell was that about?

NONNA: *(Looking down into the floor)* Forget about it.

MITTY: Forget about it? Forget About It?!?! How can I just 'forget' about something like that? Do you know what this means Nonna? Do you?

NONNA: Yes.

MITTY: Then why did you do it?

NONNA: Look. I'm… I'm sorry. Just drop it please.

(Mitty huffs. A long pause)

NONNA: I think my days are numbered, Mitty.

MITTY: Why, what are you? A calendar?

NONNA: I'm serious Mitty. I mean… just look out there.

(Stands. Mitty looks up and follows Nonna's extended finger, pointing out into the audience.)

MITTY: Another metaphor?

NONNA: Almost.

MITTY: They've never seemed this close before.

(Mitty stands and looks out into the audience.)

NONNA: I wonder if they've ever heard us?

MITTY: Doubt it. Who do you think is older?

NONNA: Us

MITTY: No, between me and you.

NONNA: There is no me and you.

MITTY: What?

NONNA: Just us and them. The everchanging 'them'.

MITTY: I wonder why they're so close this time.

NONNA: It's a metaphor.

A beautiful one. *(Smiles)*

This time we are the stars. This time they are looking above their own beautiful world. Glimpsing into ours. They are trying to discover our secrets while we comment on theirs.
I want to visit them someday.

MITTY: We're not allowed to visit them Nonna. It's forbidden. And they aren't watching us. We're not their equals. They live upon a planet. In a world of colour. We live in The White. Now come on you need to rest.

NONNA: *(Looks around)* It's night-time?

MITTY: It's night-time somewhere.

NONNA: Doesn't mean its night-time here though.

MITTY: It's just an expression, don't be stupid.

NONNA: I think you'll find everyone is entitled to be stupid.

MITTY: Yes, but some people *(raises eyebrows at NONNA)* like to abuse the privilege.

Goodnight.

(Mitty lies on the sofa, pulling a white blanket over to keep warm. Moments pass and it becomes apparent Mitty has fallen asleep. Nonna becomes quickly bored and turns to Mitty's sleeping form. Moving around the Sofa, Nonna pulls a series of ridiculous, funny faces, getting as close as possible to - but without waking Mitty. Suddenly tiring of this charade, Nonna returns to the front and sits cross-legged.)

NONNA: *(Frowns, sighs and looks out)* I bet Mitty doesn't even think you're real you know. Mitty reckons you're just a conspiracy, like the thing with our names, did you hear about that?

No, I suppose you didn't. But Mitty's always been like that. Pretending to hate me. Pretending to hate the world.

Sometimes, I wonder if you know what it's like.
Living in here. Not knowing when It'll end. When the metaphors will stop. Sometimes I think its torture. Or a purgatory of sorts. But then I catch something so beautiful and I just… just stop.

I wonder what it must be like. To be you. To observe the observers.

I guess we're like gods, me and Mitty. Always here. Always working. Always overseeing your troubles and not really doing much to help.
We have for decades. We see everything you choose to ignore, everything you choose to create. We're not allowed to process it all though. Company policy, I guess. It's too much for one partnership room to handle anyway. Creating and processing your metaphors for you is enough work as it is.

(Pause)

Mitty seems to think there was a beginning to this somewhere. Apparently, a long time ago we weren't even here. Weren't needed. Then you lot bred like rabbits and here we are. Stuck working in The White.

(Nonna seems to sense something and turns slowly. The woman has stood up at some point, just behind the Sofa and is watching with slight fascination. The pain, however, is still visible and the tears are still flowing.)

WOMAN: *(Slowly, in a hollow, flat almost whisper)* You don't remember.

NONNA: You speak?

(Nonna waits for the Woman to continue. As silence ensues Nonna edges closer to the sofa, hand outstretched ready to awaken Mitty.)

WOMAN: Don't bother, Nonna.

NONNA: But why?

WOMAN: Because there's guilt in that one.

(A new day. Mitty is staring down at the curled body of The Woman. Rolling eyes, Mitty then turns to Nonna who is sat, sulking at the front of the stage)

NONNA: *(Annoyed)* I'm telling you Mitty, she spoke!

MITTY: She didn't speak Nonna! You were dreaming again.

NONNA: This wasn't a dream Mitty!

MITTY: Honestly, what is getting into you Nonna? First you think you're feeling forbidden emotions, then your hallucinating! It's not right!

NONNA: *(Snaps and stands)* For goodness sake Mitty. They are not hallucinations!

MITTY: YES, THEY ARE. Just listen to yourself Nonna!

Do you really think she spoke? She hasn't spoken for… for… well forever!

NONNA: You have to believe me Mitts! She just said something about guilt then crawled back into the corner where she always is! I think-

MITTY: -Your over thinking is putting our jobs in jeopardy Nonna. And its Mitty for the record. Not Mitt's or whatever pathetic nickname you've invented!

NONNA: I know what I saw, Mitty.

MITTY: No Nonna, no you don't. Look, the last thing I want to do is hurt you-

NONNA: Oh, so it's on the list.

MITTY: What is?

NONNA: Hurting me.

MITTY: Seriously? Nonna, I don't know where this sudden attitude problem has come from but sort it out. Before we both lose our jobs. Or worse.

NONNA: I don't have an attitude problem. You have a perception problem.

(Still annoyed, Nonna slumps back down, clutching knees to chest.

A very long pause.)

MITTY: I have a metaphor.

NONNA: *(Suddenly excited)* Ooh go on!

(Mitty crouches behind Nonna and points out, Nonna follows his finger, enthralled.)

MITTY: See the boat out there?

NONNA: Ay, Ay captain.

MITTY: *(Rolls eyes)* See the dolphins next to them?

NONNA: They're beautiful.

MITTY: Well the way they move together, the fluidity and grace. The clicking and playfulness….

NONNA: They're like a family.

MITTY: They're an allegory for war.

NONNA: What?

MITTY: *(Still staring forward)* They click like a timer on a bomb.

NONNA: That's just how they speak!

MITTY: They're not speaking words. Or even English for that matter.

They are different. Crossing oceans and seas that don't belong to them. Never settling. Never satisfied.

NONNA: Uhm...that's because they're fish?

Look I don't know where you're going with this Mitty, but I'll go with the 'flow', I guess…. *(Laughs to self)*

MITTY: Only dead fish go with the flow Nonna.

Dead.

By the hands of a dolphin. Dead by the hands of war machines. They may smile and look friendly, but they carry the fin of a shark, the hunger of a pack. They want to consume life, not preserve it. They select their prey then drop like bombs into the bloodshed. They take joy watching death. And the humans nurture them.

(Slightly disgusted)

They call them endangered.

NONNA: *(Rolls eyes)* They are endangered Mitty! They should be protected.

MITTY: War shouldn't.

NONNA: Why? We've watched many a good war together.

Remember that big one over some land?

(Reminisces with a smile) What a season for metaphors that was.

MITTY: War isn't good Nonna.

NONNA: It's not?

MITTY: Has your time here not taught you anything?

NONNA: They need war though Mitty. They need it to settle who is right.

MITTY: War doesn't determine who is right Nonna. Merely who is left.

NONNA*: (Winces suddenly, as if a slight pain has quickly shot through the head.)*

Do you love me Mitty?

MITTY: What?

NONNA: I just processed another love metaphor…. It got me thinking. We've always witnessed love. Never questioned if we have it though.

MITTY: Why would we? We just do our job.

NONNA: I just thought… with all this time together?

MITTY: Time doesn't mean anything.

NONNA: So, you don't feel the slightest thing? Wouldn't call me anything? Like a friend or acquaintance or... or -

MITTY: - Oh, I'd call you something alright.

NONNA: *(Smiles beamingly)* Aw!

MITTY: A pain in my ass! *(Laughs)*

NONNA: Oh.

(Pause. Mitty slowly sits up realizing Nonna's sudden silence is one of sadness)

MITTY: I actually have lots of friends, you know.

NONNA: *(Chuckles with immediate doubt)* Like?

MITTY*: (Points and looks at the curled-up body of The Woman)*

Like…. Her! She likes me!

Don't you?

(They pause waiting for a response.)

MITTY: *(Hearing no reply, turns back shrugging.)* She's just shy.

NONNA: *(Laughs)* I can't believe you. I have a heart of gold I'll have you know.

MITTY: So, does a boiled egg Nonna. Doesn't mean anything.

(A loud KNOCK)

MITTY: What was that?

NONNA: What was what?

MITTY: That knock. *(Stands up, looks side to side confused)*

NONNA: What Knock?

(KNOCK)

MITTY: *(Raises finger and turns around worriedly intrigued)*

There! Did you hear it?

NONNA: Um, No.

MITTY: You must have.

(KNOCK)

See! There it is again!

(Rushes to the side wall, pressing ear against it, trying to find the source of the noise)

NONNA: (Laughs and looks forward, rolling eyes)

Ah I get it! This is one of your Knock, Knock jokes again isn't it! I love these! Shall I do one?

Knock, Knock -

(Pauses as Mitty continues to search room for source of sound)

Mitty, this is where you say, 'whose there.'

(KNOCK)

MITTY: I think it's coming from outside the room.

NONNA: Jesus, I'll finish the joke myself.

(A quieter KNOCK comes from under the flooring. Hurriedly, Mitty leaps to the floor and pushes Nonna aside, intently pressing an ear to the centre of the woollen rug as if waiting for the sound to come back.)

NONNA: Knock, Knock -

(Mitty knocks the floor trying to communicate with the source. Nonna's head whips around sharply.)

Mitty, I think I heard it!

MITTY: (Sighs) That was me, you -

Never mind, come here I think it's coming from under this.

(Gestures Nonna over)

NONNA: (*Stands then stops*)

Uh... Mitty.

(Pause)

Mitty!

MITTY: *(Waves Nonna away)*

Not now, Nonna.

(KNOCK)

NONNA: Mitty!

MITTY: I said not now!

NONNA: She's standing!

(Mitty whips around and see's the Woman, who has at some point during the knocking, stood up and is watching them intently)

MITTY: What… what do you want!?

I said, what do you want!?

NONNA: *(Pulls Mitty back by the shoulder)*

Mitty, I don't think she's going to answer you.

MITTY: (*Rips self from Nonna's grasp*)

GODDAMMIT WOMAN! Answer me! What. Do you. Want.

WOMAN: (*Blinks blankly.*) Rug
MITTY: What?

NONNA: I think she said hug!

(*Cheerily, steps forward, arms a little outstretched*)
Do you want a hug?

WOMAN: (*Blankly takes a step back*)

Rug.

MITTY: Rug, she's saying rug.

NONNA: Rug? Ooh, Is this a riddle?

MITTY: (*Bends down and starts flipping the rug over. Looks up at Nonna fleetingly.*)

You're actually a waste of two billion years of evolution, you know that righ-.

(*Mitty stops and slightly retracts away from the rug with an unreadable expression.*)

NONNA: What is it?

(*Mitty picks the rug up and turns it around so both Nonna and the audience can see the underside. Emblazoned and written obviously in blood reads 'MURDERER'*)

MITTY: Murderer.

NONNA: What the hell!

MITTY: (*Throws rug to floor and turns to The Woman in fury*)

Do you know about this?

Did you do this?

(*The woman just stares down blankly at the rug.*)

DID YOU DO THIS!

NONNA: Yelling won't help Mitty.

MITTY: How did she know this was here?

NONNA: *(Shrugs)* Lucky guess?

MITTY: This is not the time for jokes Nonna. This is serious.

NONNA: (*Bends down and returns the rug to its original position*)

Maybe you're…. over reacting?

MITTY: Over reacting? Over reacting!

NONNA, THE WORD MURDERER IS WRITTEN ON OUR CARPET!

NONNA: Maybe it's just a joke?

MITTY: How are you so calm Nonna? We hear knocking then suddenly this shows up out of nowhere!

NONNA: Look for all we know it could've been there this entire time.

MITTY: This doesn't fluster you in the slightest?

NONNA: A little, but there's no point getting worked up about it unless something else happens. We won't get answers by just panicking.

You taught me that. (*Sits down*)

MITTY: We do have answers Nonna. She knows.

(*Turns to woman angrily*)
Don't you!

NONNA: (*Shakes head*) We don't know that Mitty.

MITTY: But if you know nothing, then she must! Help me Nonna.

NONNA: Help you? How?

MITTY: She can obviously talk so…so we'll get her to spill.

NONNA: And how are you going to do that?

MITTY: (*Pauses*) The Sofa.

The Sofa will have something that'll make her talk.

NONNA: (*Rolls eyes*) Tell me if it has something stronger than nicotine will you.

MITTY: The Sofa only provides necessities Nonna, even you know that.

(*Searches the back of the Sofa*)

MITTY: For goodness sake.

(*Pulls out bottle of whisky*)

NONNA: (*Laughs and reaches up taking it out of an annoyed Mitty's grip*)

Brilliant!

(*Pops it open and takes a sip. Obviously hates the contents but swallows it anyway*)

Want a bit?

(*Head shaking, Mitty sits next to Nonna defeatedly. The Woman slowly sinks back into her fetal position.*)

MITTY: (*Softly*) This doesn't scare you even in the slightest. Not even after your dream episode the other day?

NONNA: *(Swallows another gulp and shrugs)* Not really. Dreams are scarier because they're not tangible. You can't do anything about them. Anyway, didn't you say being scared was a forbidden feeling?

MITTY: Yes but –

(With a sudden look of realization crossing Mitty's face, Mitty stands and shakes Nonna triumphantly)

Shit, Nonna you're right!

(Backs away, hands clasped around the back of head in relief)

NONNA: Well what can I say… When am I not?

MITTY: *(Points to rug)*

This must be a test! We're due a review soon, aren't we?

NONNA: *(Shudders and takes another sip)* Christ I hope not.

MITTY: It must be. There's no other explanation for it. Why have you gone quiet?

NONNA: Just thinking.

MITTY: You don't think I'm right?

NONNA: Maybe. I don't know. You just need to calm down.

(Leans down and picks up the rug, looking at it admiringly)

Aw. It's beautiful.

MITTY: What is?

NONNA: *(Lowers rug)* To see red… To see something that isn't white.

MITTY: We see colours all the time.

NONNA: Not in here we don't. Here is just white. Plain old white. Why can't it all be red or black or pink or yellow, ooh yellow is nice actually.

I wonder if the Sofa would give us some paint?

MITTY: *(Rolls eyes)* We don't have time to paint Nonna. We're behind as it is. And even if we did it certainly would not be yellow.

NONNA: Why not?

MITTY: Yellow is ugly. Anyway, the room needs to be white. You can't work in a place called 'The White' and expect it to be blue or pink or green or something.

NONNA: I didn't choose to work here.

MITTY: Neither did I. But hey you know what they say... when one door opens…

(Waits for Nonna to finish the sentence. Nonna shrugs dumbfounded)

Another closes...

NONNA: (*Shakes head and laughs*) You'd be a terrible cabinet maker.

(Pause)

MITTY: Who did you work with anyway. Before you got assigned with me?

NONNA: Worked up in the revelations department. Partner went by the name of Phenome. Was an absolute nightmare. It was so long ago though. I barely remember it.

MITTY: Was the room the same?

NONNA: Exactly. (*Yawns and nods in the direction of the Woman*)

Minus crazy lady over there.

MITTY: What was… what was Phenome like?

(Pause)

NONNA: Horrible.

Reminds me of you a tad.

MITTY: Of me?

NONNA: Only a little. You're nicer but Phenome had the same mood swings. Just... just more often. Oh, and hogged the sofa instead of occasionally sharing. I always remember being cold.

(Pause)

And alone.

(Pause)

What happened to your old partner anyway?

MITTY: It doesn't matter. Time for bed don't you think.

NONNA: If you say so.

(Goes to get off the sofa)

MITTY: No, Nonna…here. You take the sofa tonight.

NONNA: Really?

MITTY: Yeah. I uh… I slept awkwardly last night, reckon the floor might help.

NONNA: Are you sure?

MITTY: Knock yourself out.

NONNA: Well at least take the blanket!

MITTY: Then you'll be cold.

NONNA: Not if I cut it in half.

(Reaches down into the Sofa and rummages)

Come on…… there must be something in here.

(Smiles and triumphantly pulls out a pair of scissors. Nonna quickly cuts the blanket into two large halves and chucks one at Mitty.)

There! Now we'll both be warm.

MITTY: *(Looks at the blanket with a smile)*

Thank you Nonna.

NONNA: *(Cheerfully)* Goodnight Mitts.

(Nonna huddles up on the Sofa as Mitty moves to the front of the stage. Wrapping the blanket around, Mitty sits and stares into the distance. There is a very long pause as the room darkens, only leaving Mitty slightly lit whilst everything else only in shadows)

MITTY: You know what. I think you were right Nonna. You are my only friend. I may act like you annoy me but... but deep down. I think you're alright you know.

Nonna?

(Nonna snores loudly)

Typical.

(Mitty looks around and spots the cigarette pack and lighter. Reaching over, Mitty grabs the pack and opens it. Studying and rolling a cigarette between two fingers, Mitty shrugs and lights it, the flame illuminating a weary facial expression. Tossing the cigarette pack behind but keeping the lighter, Mitty takes a moment to smoke.)

WOMAN: *(Stands in silence for a moment, staring at Mitty - features hidden by the lack of lighting, with only her silhouette and form visible.)*

You're falling apart Mitty.

MITTY: *(Takes a drag and exhales slowly, staring out.)*

You're starting to do my head in.

WOMAN: You'll lose your friend.

MITTY: Acquaintance actually.

(Flicks lighter and watches the flame dance in the air)

And I know.

(Pause)

What do I call you now anyway?

WOMAN: That is unimportant.

MITTY: *(Laughs)* Apparently everything in this place is unimportant.

…And when did you even start talking?

WOMAN: When it was realized that you are still remembering.

MITTY: Was it actually expected I'd forget?

(Pause)
So, you're not a threat?

WOMAN: I'm not a friend.

MITTY: Then join me. (*Pats side*)

WOMAN: *(Hesitates but finally moves into the light and kneels down next to Mitty, clasping her hands in her lap, face expressionless but still mascara and tear stained)*

What an ugly view.

(Laughs, offers woman a cigarette, she ignores Mitty and continues staring forward)

MITTY: You know, I thought you'd be gone by now.

WOMAN: Is that why you've been ignoring me? Pretending you don't know me?

MITTY: I usually forget you're there. Some of us have a job you know.

WOMAN: You've stopped drinking.

MITTY: And you're wondering why I've gotten worse? (*Chuckles*)

Perhaps I should start again.

WOMAN: Perhaps.

(Pause)

The end is coming Mitty.

MITTY: Ah... (*Takes a drag*) you sense it too.

WOMAN: Your end is coming Mitty.

MITTY: I thought as much. What of Nonna?

WOMAN: Depends

MITTY: On what?

WOMAN: Your past.

(Pause)

MITTY: I often wonder about you. When I'm waiting for a metaphor to come. I wonder if you receive them too. I sometimes look over at you, try and figure out what you're thinking. Huddled away from the world. Not looking. Don't you miss it?

WOMAN: It is ugly.

MITTY: But it can be wonderful. *(Looks at Nonna)* Some may even say beautiful.

WOMAN: You dare call it beautiful after what you did?

MITTY: I said it 'can be'. Not 'it is'.

(Pause)

How long anyway?

WOMAN: Anyway?

MITTY: The end, how long is it away?

WOMAN: Unimportant.

MITTY: Ha, I bet they can't wait to see me gone.

WOMAN: Your sentence could be revoked.

MITTY: And what then? More metaphors? More watching? You don't understand. I have been in The White for far too long. Trust me when I say a death will be the greatest excitement I've had in years.

WOMAN: You don't deserve excitement.

MITTY: Tell me something I don't know.

(*Pause*)

WOMAN: Three cycles.

MITTY: Hm?

WOMAN: Three cycles Mitty. Three cycles. Then justice.

MITTY: (*Stubs out cigarette*) It's a date.

(Sometime late mid-day. Nonna is sat in Mitty's usual spot, throwing a small ball at the adjacent wall, letting it bounce off and catching it satisfied. Mitty on the other hand, is lying on the Sofa reading.)

MITTY: The Sofa only provides necessities Nonna, even you know that.

NONNA: *(Catches the ball and sighs)*

But it's been a long day Mitty. And I'm hungry!

MITTY: We don't get hungry Nonna.

NONNA: But did you hear the amount of food related metaphors that I had to process today? It was ridiculous Mitty. Utterly ridiculous! Some lady compared a cucumber to a... to a... You know what it doesn't matter! The point is I'm starving!

MITTY: *(Chuckles)* It literally gave you food for thought.

NONNA: *(Groans)* That's not funny! Look for once Mitty, just once can we have something edible. I just... I just want to taste something. See what it's like, you know?

MITTY: You could spend some of your meta – fortune I suppose.

NONNA: My what?

MITTY: Don't tell me you've forgotten about that as well.

NONNA: Umm…. Maybe?

MITTY: *(Sighs)* Every four years you get credit. It's not a lot but I'm sure by now you definitely have enough to buy whatever food you want from the Sofa.

NONNA: (*Stands up and walks to back of the Sofa*) Oh I think... I think I remember them explaining something about that actually.

(*Looks down at the Sofa*)

How... how do I do it again?

MITTY: Same way we do everything around here, Nonna. Telepathy.

NONNA: (*Nonna takes a moment to think then reaches down, deep into the Sofa. With a beaming smile, Nonna pulls out two large containers. With an excited smile, Nonna passes a noodle pot to Mitty*)

Here you go!

MITTY: What?

NONNA: (*Thrusts the pot into Mitty with a chuckle*) Well I wasn't going to let you sit here while I just ate.

MITTY: (*Smiles, humbled at Nonna's kindness*) Gosh. Um...

Thanks Nonna. Are you sure? I mean you spent your Meta-fortune on this... on me. Don't you want it?

NONNA: (*Sits down next to Mitty and laughs*) Just shut up and eat it Mitts. Ooh what have they given us?

MITTY: I believe they call it Chinese.

NONNA: Ooh my favourite!

What's that you've been reading anyway?

MITTY: Just a book.

NONNA: (*Laughs*) Wow really? I would never have guessed!

What's it about?

MITTY: Just these two men who go travelling and looking for work.

NONNA: Sounds boring.

Can I give it a go?

MITTY: (*Laughs*) Do you even know how to read?

(Nonna shoots a look)

Fine, yes you can read it.

(*A pause as the two tuck in with joy.*)

NONNA: Hey, I have a joke actually. What do you call friends you like to eat with?

MITTY: Nonna, we're eating. Save it for afterwar-

NONNA: Taste buds. (*Laughs*)

MITTY: (*Groans*) Go away.

NONNA: Funny right!

MITTY: (*Shrugs*) A little.

NONNA: Overheard it whilst processing yesterday.

MITTY: Oh, speaking of yesterday… I came across an interesting metaphor. Pretty much by accident. Sounded like something you'd like.

NONNA: (*Intrigued*) Yeah?

MITTY: From a dude in Texas.

NONNA: Oh, I love the Americans! Most of them anyway. Not too keen on that one gobby billionaire though.

MITTY: The orange one?

NONNA: That's the one… that ego centric, hypocritical –

MITTY: - Anyway, this Texan man was listening to the radio.

NONNA: Go on

MITTY: There was a song, it was kind of rocky, I liked it anyway-

NONNA: (*Laughs*) You liked something that wasn't Beethoven?

MITTY: Yes, but anyway the man-

NONNA: (*Leans forward*) Ooh I have a joke about Beethoven!

MITTY: I'm trying to tell you a story here.

NONNA: It's just a quick one. I promise you'll love it.

MITTY: It better be funny.

NONNA: It will! (*Places noodle pot down and leans forward*)

Okay, what noise does Beethoven hear every time he feeds his chickens?

MITTY: I couldn't possibly guess.

NONNA: (*Mimics a chicken, flapping wings and bucking head*)

Bach, Bach, Bach!

(*A pause as Mitty stares at Nonna with disapproval*)

MITTY: That was awful! And I've forgotten my damn story now Nonna.

NONNA: I could tell another joke?

MITTY: (*Looks horrified*) Heavens no. Just…. Just eat your noodles while I think.

(Pause)

Got it!

NONNA: (*Slightly excited*) Ooh go on.

MITTY: He was listening to a song and its lyrics went-

NONNA: - Oh, Mitty.

MITTY: (*Throws hands in the air defeated*)

You know what forget the damn tale!

NONNA: Just out of curiosity...

MITTY: What?

NONNA: Are you starting to feel pain?

MITTY: What do you mean?

NONNA: (*Frowns a little*) It's just... over these last few days Processing's been leaving me with these awful headaches. The metaphor enters and as I'm deciphering and reconverting it, I can feel it stinging. Almost like a burning. Is that normal?

MITTY: Probably just growing pains or something. You'll get through it. You know what they say, Where there's a will, there's a –

NONNA: Dead relative?

MITTY: -A way.

NONNA: (*Laughs*) Oh.

It's weird though. We never get pain here. Perks of the job I suppose.

MITTY: (*Quietly*) Speak for yourself.

NONNA: (*Looks concernedly at Mitty*) You feel pain?

MITTY: (*Dejectedly*) All the time.

NONNA: Do you want pain killers? I'm sure the Sofa-

MITTY: (*Laughs*) Painkillers can't cure this type of pain, Nonna.

NONNA: You need something stronger?

MITTY: (*Shakes head*) Just... Don't worry Nonna. I've put up with it for decades. Another lifetime of it is nothing.

NONNA: You're lying.

MITTY: No, I'm not.

NONNA: You're lying!

MITTY: So, what if I am?

NONNA: We don't lie to one another Mitty. I've made you promise to it hundreds of times.

MITTY: (*Pauses, uncomfortable*) Fine. It's like this head pain.

NONNA: Like mine?

MITTY: No. Inside.

NONNA: Something mental?

MITTY: I don't know.

NONNA: What's it like?

MITTY: (*Stares ahead into the dark.*)

It's... it's hard to explain. It's just like an emptiness.

NONNA: (*Confused*) Your head feels empty?

MITTY: Almost.

NONNA: But you have a brain and stuff in there. How can it feel –

MITTY: It's a metaphor.

NONNA: Oh.

(Silence)

MITTY: It swallows you.

NONNA: What does? The pain?

MITTY: *(Still staring far off, with an almost sad, depressive gaze)*

Kind of. It just… It just swallows you. Not straight away. Not whole.
Just bit by bit. It starts with doubt, you see. This little voice.
At first it sounds like a stranger. Telling you things that you'd never
think. Telling you something every day that grinds you down just
that little bit more. Then one day you realize the voice isn't a
stranger. It's you.

NONNA: (*Looks around confused*) Me?

MITTY: (*Chuckles sadly*) No not you Nonna.

You realize the voice is a part of you. And not just a part of you. As it continues it just becomes you. Defines you almost. It makes you believe that you're just a second thought. It whispers to every inch of you. Every organ. Every muscle. It tells your heart to become anxious. It tells your hands to tremble. It tells your brain it's not smart enough. It makes you feel like you're just a figure - only designed to be in someone else's story. You crawl through the days, smiling and saying 'yeah' and 'mm-hmm' because you know what it's like to carry and take on other people's troubles. You don't want them to bear the weight that you're struggling to hold

And then to even the most trained eye you look engaged, part of the conversation. You've done it so many times that you've become the perfect audience. You know what it's like to listen to a crying friend. You know what it's like to want to help so badly that it kills you seeing anyone else battle.

But then…. then the closest people, the ones who know you best - the ones who've detected change, who might have been able to save you… they become fooled you see. They think you're cured because you've started venturing outdoors, started making others happy. But all that time you're just… just a hollow mould of a person. You... you want to reveal everything to them, want to scream at them that the person in front of them is something... someone new, an override. A system failure. That they may as well be talking to a stranger. But you don't.

You just smile and say 'mm-hmm' because the voice that's taken over, the thing manifesting in there, controlling its host, it doesn't want to be detected. Doesn't want to be removed.

You soon learn that everyone is self-centered Nonna. It comes naturally. Self-preservation, Self-belief. Self-disbelief. Does a mother actually love a child because of its soul? Or does she love it because it's a part of her? Does she actually care for the thoughts in its head? The opinion it's formed of her?

You start to realize that no one really cares for another human being. We pretend we care so that we keep the role models and companions we need.

NONNA: (*Holds hand comfortingly*) That's not true Mitts. And mothers do love their kids. We've seen it. We've seen them starve so that they can eat, seen them kill to protect.

MITTY: (*Shakes head*) Yes, but we've also seen them sold Nonna. Sold for money. Abused. Left for dead. This is what I mean. How you perceive everything is changed. You meet people who you want to love, people who you want to befriend but you can't. You meet people who you'd die for, who you fall for.

Who you want to let in…to the point, it kills you that you can't because you're so unsure of the future.

Unsure if that little voice will come niggling its way back in, destroying you all over again. So, you let them go. You push them away, so they won't get hurt. So, they won't get infected, won't be near when the bomb finally goes off or before they get shot. You leave little breadcrumbs for them, a little part of you begging all the forces in the universe that they might just become bombproof, might be brave enough to kick the voice out for you. But then... then you realize that they're only human. They've got problems too. They can't help you. So you just… you just have to leave them.

(Sadly)

It's a cycle Nonna. It's a fucking cycle.

And it turns you into a monster.

NONNA: (*Smiles gently*) You're not a monster Mitty. Would a monster sit here and eat Chinese with me?

MITTY: A hungry one might.

NONNA: (*Laughs*) See Mitty things get better. I'm sure of it! I haven't been doing this job for as long as you, but I've still seen things down on that funny little planet. Things seem stormy and rough, but it never rains forever.

MITTY: It does in the rainforest.

NONNA: No, it doesn't.

MITTY: Yes, it does.

NONNA: Nope. It rains for the majority of the time, but the trees still need time to breathe. Time to grow and reach up to the sun. Ooh...Perhaps you can think of yourself as a tree in a rainforest Mitty!
Think about it. Rainforests have a canopy, right? That canopy is the front you put on. The face you show in public. And below that is darkness. That's your darkness Mitty, the voice you were on about. It lurks beneath the surface, hidden. But you'll be the tree. You'll grow, pushing up, fighting through the canopy towards the sun.

You'll always have the darkness. It's there of course but you'll have people who'll find it intriguing. They'll want to explore it. People who appreciate the darkness. They're the type of people who you need Mitty.
Explorers. Your roots will be used to the darkness. It'll make them stronger. And you're used to the rain, so you know what that means Mitty? That means you'll appreciate the sunlight just that bit more than the other trees. You'll soak it in, and you'll be green Mitty.

You'll push up and you'll be the tallest tree in the forest. I know you will.

That's a nice metaphor, don't you think?

(Nonna smiles of into the distance as Mitty looks down into the floor)

MITTY: I think… I think it's beautiful Nonna.

NONNA: Really? And Mitts…

MITTY: Yeah?

(Nonna leans to the side and wraps Mitty into a tight hug. Although Mitty resists at first, Nonna's persistence wins and Mitty gives up, hesitantly putting a hand on Nonna's back comfortingly.)

NONNA: I'll be your explorer Mitty. We'll kick that voice out.

MITTY: Thanks, Nonna.

(Pulls away and smooths down front)

(Nonna smiles and picks up the spare blanket. They both lay on the Sofa at opposite ends.)

NONNA: Goodnight Mitts.

MITTY: Goodnight Nonna.

(The pair are submerged in darkness. A very long pause signaling the passing of the night, While the odd floorboard creaks and the sofa makes a little noise from tossing and turning bodies, the room is silent. Still in complete darkness, a couple hours have passed. Suddenly, a slightly louder creak followed by a yawn)

NONNA: *(In the dark)*

Mitty I'm having a dream again.

(No reply)

Mitty, wake up.

(A pause as Nonna realizes Mitty is not on the Sofa)

Wait…Mitty are you on the floor?

Its freezing Mitts……… Come back to bed!

(A creak from the sofa as Nonna sits up)

Where's that bloody torch?

Mitty?

(Pause as Nonna switches on the torch, shining it forward into the audience)

This isn't funny!

(A sudden loud creak from a floorboard. Nonna turns slowly and shines the torch light at the back of the room.

As the light hits the wall, we hear Nonna release a sound of terror. Strung up against the wall is Mitty, in an almost crucifixion pose - arms outspread and hands nailed into the wall. Mitty's feet hang, hovering just above the floor.
As Nonna processes the horror, Mitty gasps, bare chest painfully expanding as air struggles to pass through the body. Blood trickles and seeps from gashes in the chest, and trails from the wounds inflicted by the long grey nails hammered into Mitty's hands. Body shaking in agony, Mitty's exhausted head droops with fatigue, as sweat drips from the blood-soaked hairline down to the hooked end of Mitty's nose, dripping into an ever-growing pool of blood that's gathered on the floor below. As Nonna processes the gruesome scene, The Woman appears, moving slowly, out from the darkness and into the torch light surrounding Mitty.)

NONNA: *(Crying out to the Woman)* Hey!

(The Woman ignores Nonna, almost in a cult, trance like state. As she approaches Mitty's struggling body, she turns to face it, slowly bringing her left hand to Mitty's now raised forehead. Mitty – exhaustedly- looks her in the eyes, blood trickling out of mouth and dripping down the weary neck. The Woman unfurls her fist, revealing another long metal nail. She positions the nail, holding it to Mitty's forehead. In her other hand she holds a hammer.
Nonna screams.
The woman retracts her arm ready to swing the hammer into Mitty's forehead.
At the same time, Nonna drops the torch, racing forward.

The lights go black.)

END OF ACT ONE

ACT TWO - Scene One

(The room is light again. MITTY lays on the Sofa, one arm hanging loosely off - almost touching the floor. Unconscious, Mitty's wounds have been washed and bandaged. Perched on the arm of the Sofa, NONNA is concernedly patting Mitty on the forehead with a damp cloth.)

NONNA: *(Looks down at Mitty and chuckles)*

Bet you wish you had painkillers now.

(Suddenly, with a loud whimper and a slight roll, Mitty's body awakens with a start- sitting up suddenly and scaring Nonna, who jumps away.)

NONNA: Oh my god!...

(Anxiously relieved)

Mitty!... Jesus Christ are you trying to give me a heart attack?

(Mitty ignores Nonna and looks around the room breathlessly in a panic. Chest panting and with a face of fear, Mitty tries to swing around to stand up.)

NONNA: Uh no, excuse me... What do you think you're doing?

MITTY: *(Winces, breathing through clenched teeth in pain and holds side)*

Leave me alone Nonna.

NONNA: Mitty, lie back down right now or so help me God I'll-

MITTY: *(Suddenly looks around and at Nonna with small, concerned surprise, then down at self.)*

I'm... I'm not dead?

NONNA: (*Picks up wet cloth from floor and chuckles*) Jeez... the lack of oxygen really went to your head. No. Thanks to me you'll soon be back to your miserable, narcissistic self in no time!

MITTY: (*Pain shooting across face, Mitty sighs uncomfortably then lifts up hands, inspecting the wounds*)

You sewed my hands up?

NONNA: Well I couldn't have you dying from blood loss, now could I? Surprising how big a hole can be caused by such a small nail.

MITTY: Thanks.

(*Pause as Nonna sits next to Mitty*)

NONNA: I didn't want to sew them up you know.

MITTY: Yeah, I can't imagine it was a pleasant job.

NONNA: (*Shakes head*)

Oh no that didn't bother me, I just thought it would make a fun game.

MITTY: What would?

NONNA: Having holes in your hands. That way if we ever played peek a boo, you could just put your hands in front of your eyes then–

MITTY: (*Rolls eyes*) -We never play peek a boo Nonna.

NONNA: (*Sighs*) True.

MITTY: (*Winces, looks at bandages and cloth*)

Where did you even get all this stuff from?

NONNA: The Sofa. (*Grins cheekily*) For some reason it seemed to think keeping you alive was a necessity.

MITTY: (*Weakly humbled*) Thank you, Nonna. For everything.

NONNA: Nah it was nothing. You'd do the same for me if I was ever you know... ever being nailed...

...to a wall.

(*Pauses confusedly looking at Mitty*)

Mitty, why were you being nailed to the wall?

MITTY: I don't know.

NONNA: It's not because I broke down the other day and got scared was it?

Oh Mitts, if it was... I'll never forgive myself!

MITTY: (*Shakes head assured*) That's not it.

NONNA: Then why did it happen? It scared me Mitts, I... I thought you were going to die.

MITTY: So did I.

NONNA: It was like something out of a horror film. Like she was possessed or a zombie or something!

MITTY: A zombie?

NONNA: Yeah, you know... those dead human things that eat brains.

MITTY: (*Snorts and smirks*) If they eat brains, then we know why you remained safe.

(*Pause as Mitty looks around hurriedly*)

Where… where is she anyway?

NONNA: (*Nods to behind the couch*) Still unconscious.

MITTY: Unconscious!?

NONNA: I had to get her away from you.

MITTY: So you knocked her out?

NONNA: (*Bites lip nervously*) It was a bit by accident! I kind of just jumped at her and she fell forward and knocked her head against the wall.

MITTY: Why did you do that?

NONNA: (*Mouth drops*) Seriously?

Mitty, the psycho was nailing you to the wall!!

MITTY: I suppose. Perhaps we should wake her.

NONNA: No. You need rest first. You nearly died!

MITTY: I'm fine. I can stay awake for another hour at the least.

NONNA: Mitty, I'm being serious! Bed. Or I'll knock you out too.

MITTY: Fine. Just… Just make sure you get some rest too.

NONNA: I promise! I'm just going to catch up on all the metaphors we missed. Don't want to get too far behind you know.

(*Pause*)

MITTY: There's actually something I forgot to tell you Nonna.

NONNA: Tell me?

MITTY: You know... yesterday, when I told you about the pain?

NONNA: The voice?

MITTY: I... I didn't tell you how bad it got.

NONNA: (*Smiles sympathetically*) I can imagine Mitty. It sounded like torture.

MITTY: No, Nonna... there... there was a time it got really bad.

(*Looks down sadly*)

NONNA: What do you mean Mitts?

MITTY: I did something Nonna. Something bad. And it just… It ate away at me. It ate away until there was just that emptiness.

NONNA: You're not a bad person Mitts.

MITTY: I was. I was terrible Nonna. I came to hate myself. I hated what I'd become. I wanted to erase the monster.

I couldn't do it anymore. The guilt, the thoughts... the endless torture of having to awake every morning and relive the past. I was trapped. You can't run away from your own mind.
I became tired Nonna. Tired of fighting an invisible enemy. Tired of fighting my own thoughts.
So many people think it's just about shutting up the voice…I think it's more to just keep it away. Keep it out. But it didn't work Nonna. It just didn't work. You can find ways to stifle the thoughts. Drinking. Drugs.

They don't do anything though. They just distract you for a tiny moment and then become yet another reason to hate yourself. And well… eventually fighting and hating myself just became the same thing. It became a circle Nonna.

(*Pauses*)

A circle that I tried ending.

But I failed.

I tried but something... my brain worked against me. My body wouldn't listen. Wouldn't shut itself down. The override was too strong and I just crumbled Nonna. I crumbled.

How pathetic ay?

NONNA: (*Shakes head gently*) You lived to see another day. I wouldn't call that pathetic.

MITTY: I think that's when I decided Nonna.

NONNA: Decided what?

MITTY: I'm too vain. I may come up with thousands of excuses, reasons why I didn't finish it that day. But I'm just too vain. Couldn't harm myself…. Just couldn't.

(Pause)

NONNA: Well if it's worth anything Mitts... I'm glad you didn't. *(Smiles)*

I think it was fate Mitty. Something else saw through your cracks. Saw the beauty trying to squeeze through. Your body wasn't trying to stop you from killing a monster Mitty. It was trying to help you save a hero.

MITTY: (*Wipes away a tear and smiles*) You're a good person Nonna.

NONNA: (*Smiles beamingly and chuckles*) I know. I'm the best.

Hey, remember the first day we met?

MITTY: Of course.

NONNA: I knew right then you'd be a tough one to crack.

MITTY: Why? Because I didn't laugh at your stupid joke?

NONNA: That was comedy gold actually!

MITTY: Me asking your name and you saying, "Nonna your business" is not comedy gold Nonna.

NONNA: Well I think it is.

(Sticks out tongue and stands)

MITTY: Goodnight Nonna

NONNA: Goodnight Mitts.

(Nonna makes sure Mitty is comfortable and the lights dim a little. Gathering the spare blanket, Nonna heads to the floor and sits, wrapping the blanket around tightly.

A few minutes of silence pass as Nonna's eyes shut.)

WOMAN: You hit me.

(Nonna's eyes fly open as the Woman appears, eerily standing behind the Sofa, staring blankly at Nonna. Nonna jumps up, terrified and spins around)

WOMAN: You hit mc.

NONNA: *(Scared, pointing a shaking finger at her accusingly)*

You... You stay away from me and Mitty, you hear me! We, we don't want you here!

WOMAN: You hit me.

NONNA: *(Meekly, still a little scared)* I... I'm sorry it was an accident!
I didn't mean- Hang on... why am I apologizing?!

YOU WERE THE ONE NAILING MY FRIEND TO A WALL!!

WOMAN: (*Unaffected by Nonna's outburst*) Mitty had to die. I was under instructions.

You intervened. Why?

NONNA: Mitty is my friend! And no one ever deserves to just die you psycho!

WOMAN: (*Blankly*) The day has come.

NONNA: What day?

WOMAN: Justice.

NONNA: (*Shakes head perplexed*) Are you out of your mind?

WOMAN: Tamper with the Highers' creation. This is the price one pays.

NONNA: (*Nervously afraid*) Just, stay … Stay away from my friend. U-Understand? I don't know what the hell you're on about, but you leave my friend out of it.

Okay?

(*Pause*)

WOMAN: You've forgotten.

NONNA: Forgotten what?

WOMAN: You don't remember.

NONNA: (*A little agitated*) Well are you going to tell me?

WOMAN: What is your first memory Nonna?

NONNA: I….

WOMAN: You don't remember do you.

NONNA: I used to work in Revelations downstairs but –

WOMAN: -That is where you began?

NONNA: I guess so? Is that my first memory?

WOMAN: Presumably. It is unimportant.

NONNA: I'm so confused.

WOMAN: Why did you move here?

NONNA: I asked for a transfer. I didn't like my colleague… Where is this going exactly?

WOMAN: And you met Mitty on your first day?

NONNA: Yes but-

WOMAN: But you didn't meet me.

NONNA: Well no... You came much later. We just woke up one morning and there you were. We tried everything to get you to talk. It shook Mitty up good and proper. Probably hadn't seen anything like it before. I mean, I haven't.

(Pause)

WOMAN: What do you know about Mitty's past Nonna?

NONNA: Mitty's past? Well… Well, Mitty's always worked in metaphors…

WOMAN: You don't remember anything about your predecessor?

NONNA: (*Shrugs*) Mitty's never really talked about his old partners. There was this one time though. Where he spoke about the one just before me. Just some woman. Really good with metaphors though apparently.

WOMAN: (*Almost bitterly*) 'Just some woman.'

NONNA: Yeah! Just… Just… (*Stops slowly and looks bewildered.*)

Some woman.

(*The two stare at each other dead in the eyes for a couple seconds then Nonna gasps*)

You? You're Mitty's old partner?

(*The Woman nods solemnly*)

NONNA: What...... I don't understand?

(*Shakes head confused*)

How? You-

(*Stops*)

Why didn't Mitty tell me?

WOMAN: That is unimportant.

NONNA: Unimportant? Unimportant?!

MITTY'S SUPPOSED TO BE MY BEST FRIEND!

WOMAN: Shush.

NONNA: Don't shush me, lady!

WOMAN: If you want to hear the truth, you will remain quiet. Mitty must sleep.

NONNA: (*Stops confused*) Must sleep? And what truth? How can I even trust you?

WOMAN: Because I was there Nonna.

(Pause)

I was there when Mitty visited the humans.

NONNA: H... Humans?

Mitty hasn't been amongst humans... We're not allowed out of here!

WOMAN: (*Gestures forward*) Sit Nonna.

And you'll learn everything.

(The room is shrouded in complete darkness.)

MITTY: (*Voice croaking through the shadows*) Nonna?

(Silence)

Nonna are you awake?... My throat really hurts. Can you get me some water?

Nonna?

(A pause as a voice breaks through the quiet)

WOMAN: Your friend is gone.

(The lights flash on as Mitty sits up in a panic. The Woman stands at the end of the Sofa, staring at Mitty almost blankly.)

MITTY: (*Winces in pain and stands up in shock.*)

What the hell is going on!?

WOMAN: Your friend is gone.

MITTY: Nonna is gone?

WOMAN: You have a choice.

MITTY: (*Confused*) Where is Nonna?

WOMAN: You have a choice.

MITTY: (*Stands up apprehensively*)
I swear to God if you have harmed-

WOMAN: Nonna is safe.

MITTY: Then where the fuck is-

WOMAN: You have a choice.

MITTY: (*Angrily, through gritted teeth, holding side in pain.*)

Tell me where Nonna is, and I'll make the bloody choice!

WOMAN: Nonna is witnessing history.

MITTY: What?

WOMAN: Nonna is witnessing your history.

MITTY: *(Pales with aghast)*

You... you sent Nonna back?

WOMAN: *(Nods)* To witness what you did.

MITTY: How? *(Turns head, looking around for a door)*

But… but you said-

(Pauses in horrified realization)

Nonna can't see what I did…! You have to stop this!

Nonna…

Nonna could be in danger!

WOMAN: *(Shrugs)* Exactly. I lost everything because of you. I tried killing you.
Nonna intervened. Now Nonna is a part of your end. I warned you Mitty. I told you Nonna's fate depended on your past.

MITTY: *(Frustrated)* You're using Nonna to get back at me? Look, you know I didn't mean to… to…

WOMAN: (*Angrily*) To rip my happiness away from me? To tear my family in two!? To kill my beautiful... my beautiful...

(*Bites inside of cheek and turns head slightly to the side, trying to prevent Mitty from seeing the anguish cross her features*)

My beautiful little girl...

(*Pause as Mitty watches her crumble*)

MITTY: Do The White know about this?

WOMAN: Yes. And they are offering you a choice.

MITTY: Wait... You? You work for them now? So that's what you've been doing. Spying on us!?

WOMAN: I've been waiting.

MITTY: For what?

WOMAN: Your sentence to end.

MITTY: Why?

WOMAN: In return for information and carrying out your punishment, they will reunite me with my daughter.

MITTY: (*Confused*) But how? Your daughter...She's...she's dead.

WOMAN: (*Face floods with an anguished rage*) Because of you Mitty! Because of you!

And you had the nerve to pretend like nothing happened. You didn't even tell your friend!

MITTY: (*Looks down regretfully*) I wanted to tell Nonna. I really did. I could just... I could never bring myself to it. Nonna saw the world as beautiful. I wanted to keep it that way.

WOMAN: What did you think you could do Mitty? Sit there and just start again? Carrying on making metaphors like nothing happened?

MITTY: You know I regret what happened. (*Shakes head with guilt*) Just… Leave Nonna out of it. Nonna is innocent.

WOMAN: No, Nonna was. (*With slight disgust*)

Until you started running your mouth. Talking about feelings and jokes and sadness.

MITTY: Nonna introduced the jokes not me. And as for sadness you know why that is perfectly justified.

WOMAN: (*Laughs mirthlessly*)
Sadness? Sadness!? You know nothing of sadness Mitty.

Nothing! Do you hear me?!

Sadness is not sitting depressed on a floor somewhere or wallowing in guilt. Sadness is seeing your child's dead body float away then sink and not... not being able to do anything... anything to stop it.

She sank Mitty.

Sank to the bottom of the ocean. Then washed up on to the shore. Like another piece of plastic. Like another piece of rubbish discarded by the world because she was seen as an inconvenience.

You put that image there Mitty.

You're the reason my baby… My baby was torn from me. The waves tried bringing her home. To me. To the world. The waves tried showing the world the evil they were ignoring.

(*Wipes away an angry tear*)

And what did the world do? They did nothing Mitty. NOTHING!

They let more babies and beautiful, beautiful children die by the dozen! And you have the audacity to sit there and pretend you had nothing to do with it!

(*Pauses as she tries to collect herself*)

She died. That was my baby Mitty. MY BABY!!

(*Sits down on the sofa, tears flowing*)

MITTY: (*Runs heads through hands beseechingly*) I… I can't begin-

WOMAN: Stop Mitty.

Nothing you say will change what you've done. You never had children. All that time on Earth. You barely socialized with them. Didn't know love or loss. Didn't know family. *(Pause. Mitty looks guilty at the floor and sits down next to the Woman)*

MITTY: (*Breathes with a tired sigh*) What did you tell Nonna?

WOMAN: Everything.

MITTY: From the beginning?

WOMAN: The very start. I told Nonna how you were young. It doesn't justify your actions, but I spoke of your youth. How The White and The Highers made you the very first Metaphor Processor.

How you then taught me everything.

MITTY: What did Nonna say?

WOMAN: Just laughed. Laughed and said you looked your age.

(*Pause*)

I described what it was like before. How only the divine had the power to compare, the power to experience. How you pleaded with The White to give humans the ability. How you were rejected every time.

And how eventually you got so frustrated you disobeyed them. How you fled to Earth and poisoned the minds of humanity.

MITTY: I didn't poison their minds.

WOMAN: Yes, you did. And you dragged me along!

MITTY: You didn't exactly stop me! And you had fun. You fell in love. You had a family!

WOMAN: I was young! Wanted adventure. To see the world. I should've stopped you.

(Pause)

I told Nonna how you shared the secret of metaphorical creation. How you thought you were giving them a gift. Consciousness you called it. An awakening.

MITTY: (*Looks down woefully then stands. Reaching deep into the Sofa, Mitty fumbles around then pulls out a bottle of wine. Frowning and sitting back down, Mitty sadly takes a swig.*)

I really thought I was helping them you know.

I saw them before, and they were just... just empty reflections of the divine. Primitive and hollow. But there was always something more to them. They weren't entirely like the other animals. They were intelligent. Protective.

Caring.

They nurtured the world around them but... but weren't appreciating it. I wanted them to see what we could see. The beauty in the birds, the calmness of the sea. The rising and setting of the sun.

I wanted them to not just pass flowers or trees, but really experience them, to be conscious and compare. I wanted them to feel the beauty of creation…. To experience the world they called home. And they loved it. They started travelling, inventing. I wanted them to not just perceive the world but use it to illuminate their thoughts. And they did.

They actually did.

In centuries to come they started relating the beauty of flowers to the beauty of love…They said the song of a nightingale was that of a human lullaby! I thought I'd actually achieved something… something….

(Looks for a word to finish the sentence)

WOMAN: Nonna called it beautiful.

MITTY: (*Takes a sip and chuckles sadly*) Nonna calls everything beautiful.

WOMAN: You were blind Mitty.

MITTY: I know.

WOMAN: You should've noticed. The moment they supposedly bit into an apple; the moment snakes became sinful.

The moment money became happiness, when beauty became defining. When evil entered their heads.

When the metaphors stopped being beautiful.

When intelligence became status and ownership became greed. When execution became entertainment. You were so caught up in your ridiculous pride. In your own self-admiration. You thought you were a God. You walked the earth, tainting their history. You were selfish Mitty. Selfish.

And you stupidly gave that power to the humans. I began seeing it from the start. But I ignored it. I ignored it because it didn't affect me. I was having too much fun. Exploring freedom. It got worse, but I had made my own slice of paradise, so I barely noticed.

I had a child. A husband. Friends.

I had actually convinced myself I was one of them. I had almost forgotten about you. Didn't ever even check up on you to see if you were actually still around. You may have travelled further west and ended up in England, but I stayed with my family. In Africa Mitty.

But things changed.

The humans started dividing Mitty. Brother on brother. Politician on politician. They fought. They wanted things that were destroying others. They stole oil from the orangutans, stole fish from the sea. They stole blood from other humans by enslaving them and stole land from natives.

Your metaphors made their way across the sea. Across to Syria where the West were trying to steal our land, where dictators were trying to steal our minds. Your metaphors called the West safe. Said Europe would want us. Save us.

We were told the West is safety.

The West is security.

The West is happiness.

But they feared for their jobs. Their economy. They were told the fleeing innocents were monsters. That we were strange. Different. They were told we were the enemy. They didn't want us. Wouldn't even shelter our young. They abandoned us.

We thought the price we were paying was worth it.

(Pauses shaking her head sorrowfully)

But it wasn't Mitty. It wasn't safe.

(Swallows tears) The White saved me, took me back. Luck saved my husband.

But who saved my girl Mitty?

Who heard her cries as the wind dragged her away? As the water filled her tiny throat… As she looked for her mama?...

(*Hoarsely, looks up accusingly*) Your metaphors killed her Mitty. And they continue killing. There are still children, women, men trying to flee that place. Their hearts are filled with empty promises of love and a new beginning. But they aren't wanted.

(*Weakly*) They are dying.

MITTY: (*Tears rolling down face*) I... I didn't mean for it to get out of hand. The humans weren't supposed to abuse it. To twist it!

Metaphors were meant to help them. I… I should've realized.

(*Shakes with remorse*) I was a monster.

WOMAN: (*Looks, eyes piercing into Mitty*) You still are Mitty. The only thing keeping that killing machine suppressed is that ridiculous partner of yours.

You don't belong in The White. You don't belong in the space between words.
You don't see the beauty in metaphors because you've seen the damage they cause. You're just a killing machine. The origin of all sin.
The White have had time to consider your fate and you will pay for every bad metaphor uttered. Every sin they've dealt. The humans will keep the ability to create metaphors. It is down to them whether they continue to abuse it.

MITTY: (*Shakes head*) Nonna isn't just a ridiculous partner. Nonna is my friend!

WOMAN: The fool can't process half as well as I could, and you know it.

MITTY: Nonna is a better partner than you ever were!

WOMAN: I'd be careful Mitty. I can still trap your friend in the past. The White told me to unleash hell on you Mitty. Hell.

MITTY: And how are you planning on doing that exactly?

WOMAN: The White are prepared to make you a deal. You see, they have a witness now. A witness to the destruction. The deaths, the evil you caused. They have a pawn.

MITTY: Nonna?

WOMAN: By now Nonna will have seen everything. But The White have a problem. Who is to say the idiot won't talk?... Won't give up your little secret?

MITTY: Nonna would never-

WOMAN: Ah, ah… but we don't know that for sure.

So, you have a choice. Upon Nonna's return, the truth will have to be erased. And it will happen.

Just the method of how exactly, well that's up to you.

MITTY: What do you mean?

WOMAN: I mean you have to choose.

You have two options. Either terminate yourself and The White will allow Nonna to live and continue working as a Metaphor Processor. All events and memories will be removed from Nonna's head, so that there are no witnesses to the past. Oh, and a new partner will be introduced as your replacement.

MITTY: (*In a hollow, defeated whisper*) The other option?

WOMAN: Kill Nonna yourself.

So that there are no witnesses to your past. You can start afresh - a new partner and you can keep your meta-fortune. You can go on like nothing happened and live out your days creating metaphors.

MITTY: (*Stands, speechlessly frightened*)

Are you crazy? That's the choice I have to make? My life or Nonna's?

WOMAN: Yes.

MITTY: (*Backs into the wall fretting fearfully and shaking head*) I… I can't just kill my friend. I won't do it. I won't.

(*Pauses, trying to stop shaking and steady breathing*)

And I won't just off myself without... without...

WOMAN: Saying goodbye?

MITTY: Yes. (*Takes a long drink*)

WOMAN: It's not your deal to deny. You committed the crime; this is your punishment.

MITTY: How would terminating Nonna even benefit The White anyway? Are they insane?

WOMAN: Oh Mitty. The White can replace Nonna in a heartbeat. Your original sentence was just too easy. There are far worse and lengthier ways to destroy a person than simple execution.

MITTY: You can't do this.

WOMAN: Oh, I can. It's really quite easy. It's necessary.

MITTY: (*Angrily indignant*) This is not necessary!

WOMAN: I think the Sofa would have to disagree with you! Go on. Go check it.

MITTY: The Sofa?

(Mitty winces in pain and turns to the Sofa. Rummaging deep, Mitty very slowly pulls out a revolver. Staring at it with an unreadable sadness, Mitty turns it around in his hand, studying the weapon.)

WOMAN: The truth has to be erased Mitty. One way or another.

MITTY: *(Looks up and points it at the Woman)* What if I refuse.

WOMAN: Then you will both be executed. Immediately and not pleasantly.

MITTY: All... *(gestures around shakily with the gun)*

All this... all this so you can get your daughter back?

WOMAN: I'd do anything to hold my girl again.

MITTY: But... but I can't kill Nonna...I won't.

I WON'T KILL NONNA.

I can't!

WOMAN: Then you must be prepared to die.

MITTY: I... I... Nonna was wrong. I am a monster. I don't deserve to...to...

(Loses it)

This... THIS ISN'T FAIR.

(Kicks sofa and slams around, sobbing into the wall. Smacking it with palms.)

I can't... I can't
(Shaking)

I can't do it. I won't….

(*Slumps down the wall, crying into it debilitated by distress.*)

I won't.

WOMAN: I will leave in a minute. I will leave and Nonna will return. You will have thirty seconds to make your decision. If no decision is reached you will both be terminated. You must choose Mitty. There is no compromise.

Goodbye Mitty.

(*The Woman bows her head and walks to the back of the room. Mitty pushes away from the wall, staring at the gun in hand and takes a few steps backwards into the centre of the room. The Woman presses herself against the back wall and repeats her movement sequence. This time her body does not glide along the smooth surface of the wall but rather molds into it, searching and grabbing into the other side. In a slow interchanging of bodies, The Woman is pulled through while a seemingly enthusiastic Nonna returns, bounding in and stands, beaming behind the Sofa.*

Breathlessly, Nonna looks wide eyed around, comically adorned in various typical tourist items. Spotting Mitty, Nonna gasps and smiles widely remaining fixated on the spot)

NONNA: Oh Mitty! You won't believe the time I've had! Its everything I dreamed it would be. I can't believe you never talked about it- Mitty?

(*Pauses*)

Mitty, Is everything okay?

(Mitty stares at the gun in hand, a tear rolling down and dripping on to the floor below.

Mitty sighs, shoulders shaking from pressure and turns very slightly, just catching Nonna's eyes.

The lights go black

A Gunshot is fired.)

ACT TWO - Scene Four

(The room remains in darkness, uncertainty building. When the lights finally fade in, MITTY sits, staring out. Rocking back and forth, Mitty looks transfixed, distant. As seconds pass, a tear starts to trail down Mitty's face, dropping on to the floor below.

The silence is suddenly disturbed by hearty groans and the sound of something being sprayed.

A head pops up from behind the sofa. **THE INDIVIDUAL**, *looks intellectual - pompous yet a little boring and with a sigh, gives Mitty a disgusted yet slightly comical look and bends back down, triumphantly picking up a bottle of detergent spray.)*

INDIVIDUAL: Ah! I think that's done the trick. The carpet will be clean in no time! Couldn't stand living with that stain there! I wouldn't be able to sleep at night knowing the room wasn't perfectly white. Honestly, can you not clean up after yourself? It's ridiculous Mitty, utterly ridiculous. I mean just look at these Chinese containers. Look at the litter!

(Pauses, fixing glasses by pushing them further up nose)

What a weird stain though. My old room had nothing like it. It was kind of brown but not like mud though.

(Silence)

MITTY: (*A whisper*) It was blood.

INDIVIDUAL: Blood!?

MITTY: My blood.

INDIVIDUAL: (*Scoffs*) Well you could've cleaned it up. Honestly, you're lucky the Sofa provided carpet cleaner otherwise you would be licking it up! How did you even get that much blood in here? This is beyond excusable! What do you have to say for yourself?

MITTY: There's another puddle of it over there.

(The Individual huffs and looks by the arm of the Sofa, spotting more blood and letting out a frustrated sigh)

INDIVIDUAL: Don't tell me that's your blood as well?

(Pause)

MITTY: (*A hoarse, hollow whisper*) No. No, It's not.

(Another tear falls)

It's from an old friend.

INDIVIDUAL: Well you could've at least told me before I thought I was done. Now I'll be up all-day scrubbing when I could be processing!

(Looks around the room sharpish then spots Mitty's book, laying discarded on the floor)

What's this? (*Picks up novel*)

(Disgusted) A book?

A book? Here In the White? What a thought! It's almost scandalous!

Is this yours?

(Sits back on the sofa, analyzing the novel)

What is it even about? Is it like a processing manual or something? I guess it would be excusable then.

(Flips through the pages and squints down, tutting)

Jesus Mitty, there's even drops of blood in here too! Is there anything, anything you didn't get blood on? Ah there's the title!

Let's see...

'Of Mice And Men.'

'Of Mice And Men?'

What a ridiculous title. You actually read this garbage? What's it about anyway?

(No reply.)

I suppose it doesn't matter.

(Gets up and crouches near Mitty's ear, looking out into the audience.)

How can one even compare a mouse to a man? What an utterly preposterous notion. Mice are vermin… They just steal from supplies that aren't theirs, they jump on ships and bring disease to other cultures and scare young children from their rooms…

Men on the other hand…

Well, the differences are crystal clear.

(Stands back up and taps Mitty on the back of the head with the book, looking around the room in thought.)

Actually! I suppose… (*Laughing*) I suppose there's one thing they both have in common.

It's a bit of a joke. Want to hear it?

MITTY: (*Defeatedly*) If you must.

INDIVIDUAL: What do mice and men have in common?

(Mitty stares blankly ahead.)

INDIVIDUAL: (*With a horrible snorty laugh*)

They both run around…. Hunting for holes!

(*Laughs incredibly excessively at the bad joke, snorting hilariously and sits down at the side of the sofa. Breathlessly, he calms himself and looks over at Mitty.*)

Jesus, you are a miserable one!

(*Pause*)

What are you even looking at anyway?

(*Pause*)

MITTY: Just…Just a metaphor.

(*Pauses, sadly smiling to self*)

And it's beautiful.

THE END

About the Author

Living in South Wales but learning at Lancaster University, Amber Taylor is an English literature and theatre undergraduate. Whilst this is her first published work, Amber has written several plays and often uses the pastime as a creative outlet. Her love for theatre has always been a strong one and she has dabbled in amateur directing, producing, writing and acting. She hopes to pursue a career in theatrical arts after university and can't wait to see what the future holds.